ART'S SUPPLIES

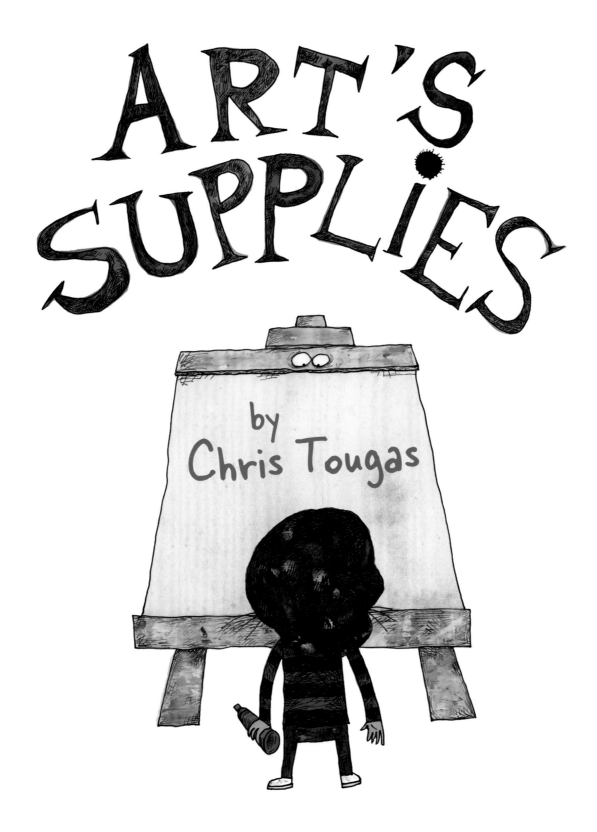

by
Chris Tougas

ORCA BOOK PUBLISHERS

"It's not my fault!" Art declared.
"My supplies have a mind of their own!"

The paper started it by inviting everyone
to her pad for a party. Things got crazy fast.

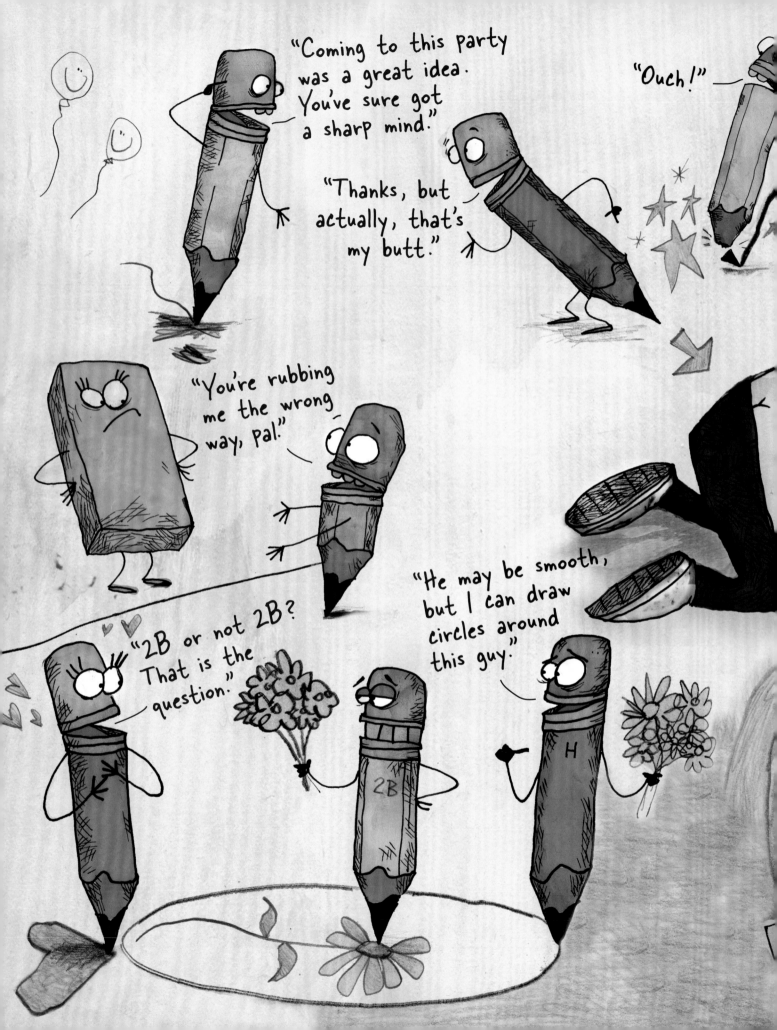

The pencils led the way. The eraser almost stopped the party but decided not to cross that line.

Next the crayons rolled in with some fun ideas.
Those guys sure know how to think outside the box.

The markers all agreed that they FELT great.

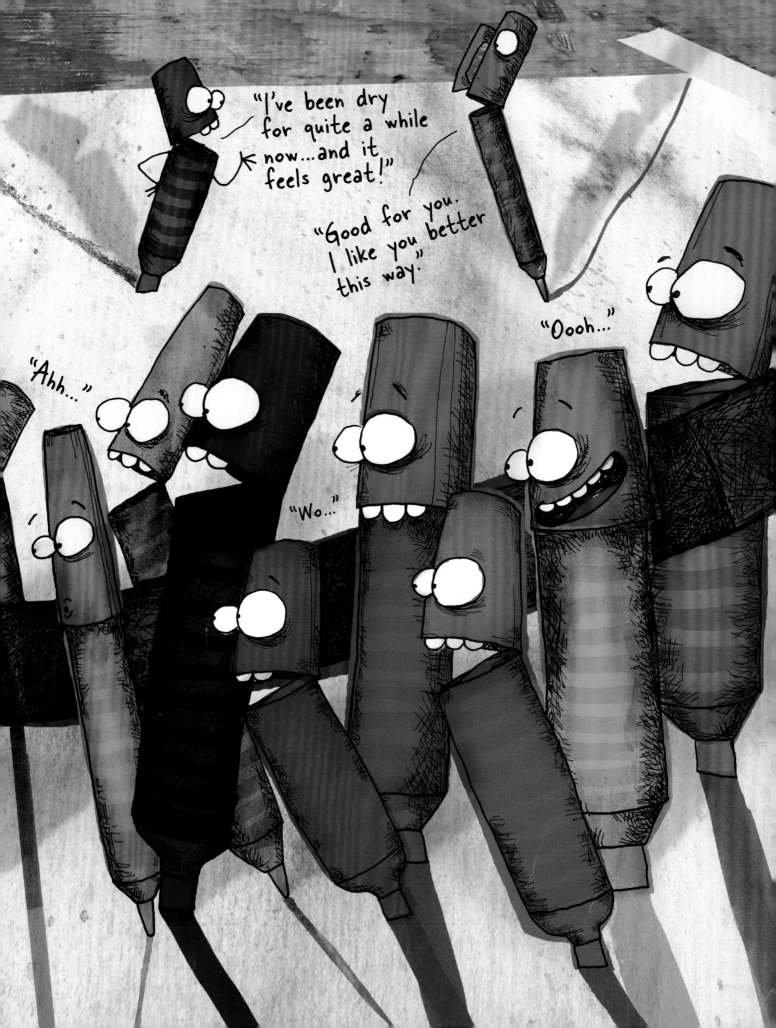

Then the pastels arrived.
They blended in smoothly.

"Anybody want to
take a dip?"

Ink arrived with a splash
and left a lasting impression.

"What's the one thing an artist can't draw? ...A good wage!"

"Why did the paint come home from work so sad? ...He was just canned!"

"Why did the large painter go to the paint store? ...He wanted to get thinner!"

The scissors were cutting jokes all night long.
They really had the tape rolling.

Things were getting pretty out of control, but the glue held everything together.

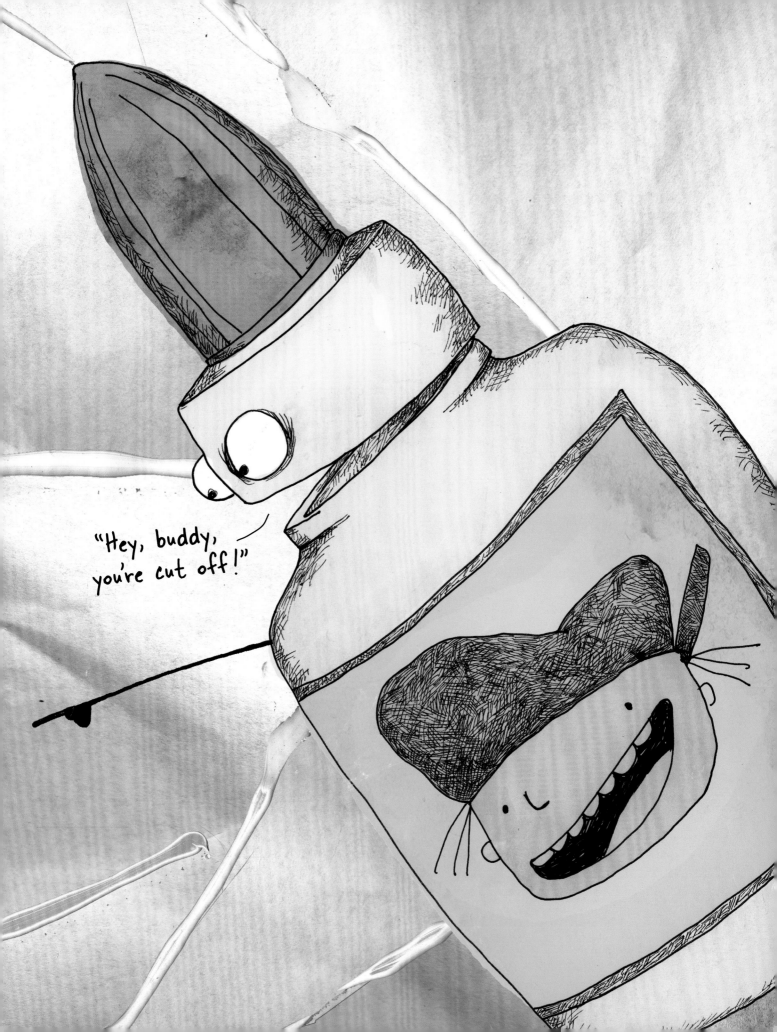

Just when I thought it was over,
the paints arrived.

The other brushes loved the idea
and jumped right in.

The pallet knife arrived and really mixed things up.

Things were getting pretty crazy, so we all remembered to have lots of water.

"Art's a splash!"

So you see, we've been too busy to clean up.

For Dad — Artist, mentor and best friend.

Library and Archives Canada Cataloguing in Publication

Tougas, Chris
Art's supplies / written and illustrated by Chris Tougas.

ISBN 978-1-55143-920-4

I. Title.

PS8589.O6774A78 2008   jC813'.54   C2007-906370-5

First published in the United States, 2008
Library of Congress Control Number: 2007939503

Summary: Art's art supplies throw a party, play with puns and get creative.

Orca Book Publishers gratefully acknowledges the support for its publishing programs
provided by the following agencies: the Government of Canada through
the Book Publishing Industry Development Program and the Canada Council
for the Arts, and the Province of British Columbia through the BC Arts Council
and the Book Publishing Tax Credit.

Cover artwork: Chris Tougas
Design: Teresa Bubela

ORCA BOOK PUBLISHERS
PO Box 5626, STN. B
VICTORIA, BC CANADA
V8R 6S4

ORCA BOOK PUBLISHERS
PO Box 468
CUSTER, WA USA
98240-0468

www.orcabook.com
Printed and bound in China.

11 10 09 08 • 4 3 2 1